Jacqueline

BIRTHDAY
JOURNAL

ILLUSTRATED BY
NICK SHARRATT

DOUBLEDAY

GW00870042

What's your favourite day of the year? I'm sure you'd choose your own birthday! It's so exciting to celebrate your special day with family and friends. I love to see birthday balloons bobbing in the air, gifts wrapped in shiny paper and coloured ribbons, and a fantastic creamy birthday cake complete with candles. I often write about birthdays in my books, and enjoy choosing each party theme and type of cake!

The Birthday Journal is a perfect way to plan your own birthday. There are delicious recipes, ideas for special home-made presents, brilliant birthday puzzles and a different party idea for each month. There's also lots of space for you to write about every single party you go to throughout the year.

Jacqueline Wilson

♡ MY BIRTHDAY ♡

This year I'll be _____ years old.

My birthday will fall on a _____

I will/won't be going to school on my birthday this year.

I celebrated my last birthday by _____

_____

with _____

_____

My favourite presents were _____

_____

This year I'd like to celebrate my birthday by _____

_____

_____

with _____

_____

_____

My perfect present would be _____

_____

_____

with a _____

_____ flavoured birthday cake!

♡ MY FAVOURITE ♡ BIRTHDAY MEMORY

Birthdays are such fun, and you probably have lots of brilliant memories from all your birthdays. What's your very favourite? Maybe your parents or friends threw you a fantastic party? Perhaps you went to a special restaurant, or ate the most delicious home-made birthday treats? Maybe your birthday memory is from someone else's birthday — your mum or dad, brother or sister, or best friend!

_____

_____

_____

_____

_____

_____

_____

_____

_____

_____

_____

_____

_____

♡ A BIRTHDAY ♡ BRAINSTORM!

When you think about your birthday, what words and pictures come into your head? Do you think about special surprises you've had, lovely presents you've received, or a particular moment you'll always remember? In the space below, write down or draw everything that springs to mind! Tracy has started you off . . .

♡ MY BRILLIANT ♡ BIRTHDAY PLAN!

How are you going to celebrate your birthday this year? Now's your chance to plan the details and make it the best birthday ever! Where would you like to spend the day? At the cinema, the swimming pool, your favourite restaurant — or even at home, having a yummy picnic in your own garden? Think about who you'll invite, the music you'll choose, the games you'll play and the food you'll eat!

_____

_____

_____

_____

_____

_____

_____

_____

_____

_____

_____

_____

★ MY GUEST LIST ★

_____

_____

_____

_____

_____

_____

_____

_____

★ MY YUMMY BIRTHDAY MENU ★

_____

_____

_____

_____

_____

BRILLIANT BIRTHDAY BAKERY!

Here are four tempting treats for you to make on your own birthday, or for your friends! They'd all make lovely presents, wrapped up in a pretty box and tied with a silk ribbon or bow.

★ SAPPHIRE'S SCRUMMY STICKY SQUARES ★

INGREDIENTS:
50g unsalted butter • 300g marshmallows
200g Rice Krispies

(Serves twelve – two squares each)

1. Line a deep, square or rectangular baking tin with greaseproof paper.

2. Melt the butter gently in a large pan.

3. Add the marshmallows and cook, stirring well until they are completely melted.

4. Remove from the heat and pour in the Rice Krispies, mixing gently with a wooden spoon.

5. Tip the mixture into the baking tin, pressing down firmly with the wooden spoon. Don't worry if it looks a little bit uneven – the mixture will be super-sticky!

6. Leave to cool, then cut into 24 squares.

7. Enjoy! These are delicious with a glass of cold milk or milkshake.

★ TRACY'S TOFFEE TREATS ★

INGREDIENTS:
5 large bananas, chopped into thin slices
10 digestive, hobnob or shortbread biscuits,
broken into small crumbly pieces
1 tub vanilla ice cream
50g nuts (almonds, hazelnuts or pecans)

FOR THE TOFFEE SAUCE:
250g caster sugar • 150ml double cream
50g unsalted butter, softened at room temperature

(Serves ten)

1. Preheat the grill to high. Spread the nuts onto a baking tray and place under the grill for two minutes until lightly toasted. Be careful not to leave them too long, as nuts burn very easily. Take them out, put them to one side and let them cool down.

2. In small dishes, place a scoop of ice cream, and top each one with a handful of banana slices and biscuit pieces.

3. Tip the caster sugar into a frying pan and add 4–5 tablespoons of cold water. Place over a medium heat and stir gently until the sugar has dissolved. Then turn up the heat and allow the mixture to bubble for 5 minutes until it starts to turn into a sticky sauce.

4. Remove from the heat and carefully mix in the cream and the butter. Allow to cool slightly.

5. Sprinkle the toasted nuts over the ice cream, banana and biscuit, and add a generous dollop of toffee sauce. Tuck in!

★ CAM'S COCOA-CREAM CAKE ★

INGREDIENTS:
150g unsalted butter • 250g caster sugar
25g cocoa powder • 4 eggs
300g self-raising flour • 100ml double cream

FOR THE TOPPING:
25g cocoa powder • 300g icing sugar
50g butter • 50ml double cream

(Serves twelve)

1. Line a deep cake tin with greaseproof paper and
switch the oven to 180°C.

2. Melt the butter gently in a pan. Stir in the sugar
and cocoa powder until smooth, then whisk in
the eggs. Finally add the cream and stir well.

3. Tip the flour into a sieve and gently shake
into the butter mixture.

4. Pour into the cake tin, making sure it's not too full!
Bake for 45 minutes and then set aside to cool down.
Now it's time to prepare the topping! Melt the rest of
the butter gently in a pan, and add the cocoa powder,
icing sugar and double cream, stirring well until
it's smooth.

5. Carefully spread the topping on the cake with a spoon.
You can use a knife to decorate the topping with
swirls and patterns here, if you like!

6. Add candles and get ready to sing
'HAPPY BIRTHDAY'!

★ BEAUTY'S BROWNIE BITES ★

INGREDIENTS:
350g chocolate • 85g plain flour
3 large eggs • 250g brown sugar
1 teaspoon bicarbonate of soda

(Serves ten)

1. Turn the oven to 160°C.

2. Take a shallow cake tin and, using a piece of kitchen roll, add a thin layer of butter to the base, so that your brownies don't stick.

3. Carefully melt the chocolate and butter in the microwave, and stir together.

4. Whisk the eggs, then add the sugar and mix well.

5. Gently add the chocolate mixture. Then shake in the flour and bicarbonate of soda, a little bit at a time. Stir gently until you have a smooth mixture.

6. Pour into the tin, pop in the oven and leave for 30 minutes.

7. Leave on a wire rack to cool for at least an hour. Then carefully cut into squares, and eat immediately – the brownies should be warm and fudgy in the middle!

♡ ENJOY A SUPER ♡ SLEEPOVER!

Sleepovers are a brilliant, fun way to celebrate
your birthday with your best friends.
Here are some top tips!

★ SLEEPOVER ESSENTIALS ★

Make sure your friends all bring these important items:
Pyjamas or a nightie
A dressing gown and slippers
A toothbrush
A pillow and sleeping bag
A favourite teddy or cuddly toy
Spare clean clothes for in the morning

★ MAKEOVERS ★

This is a great way to start the party, and will have
everyone giggling in no time! Take it in turns to
try new make-up and hairstyles out on each other.
When you've finished, ask your mum or dad to take
a group photo, for a perfect memento of the night!

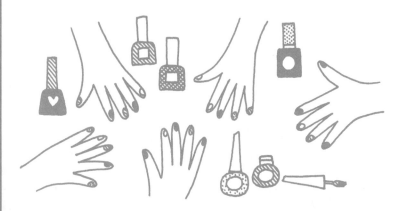

★ SPOOKY STORIES ★

If everyone's feeling brave, cuddle up in your sleeping bags, switch off the lights and take it in turns to tell your scariest story. You can even turn it into a competition, and give a little prize to the person who tells the best one!

★ MIDNIGHT FEAST! ★

What could be better than having a midnight feast at a sleepover? You don't even have to wait until midnight! You could try making some of the yummy treats on the previous pages, or ask every friend to bring along something tasty for everyone to share. Switch off the lights, turn on your torches, then spread the goodies out on a blanket and tuck in!

♡ PERFECT PRESENTS! ♡

If you want to give a friend or a member of your family a special or unique birthday present this year, you could try making something yourself.
Here are some ideas:

★ HOME-MADE TREATS ★

Quick, easy and very yummy! You could choose from chocolate brownies, cookies, cupcakes, or a big fat sponge cake. Then decorate whatever you make with icing, chocolate buttons or fruity jelly sweets.

★ A PHOTO COLLAGE ★

All you need is one large piece of stiff cardboard – A3 size is perfect. Collect photos of yourself and your friend together, along with fun pictures and words ripped out of your favourite magazines, and stick them all down on the cardboard. If there are any blank spaces left, fill them in with scraps of pretty material, ribbon, feathers, or even glittery nail varnish. Your friend can hang your creation on her bedroom wall!

★ A STORY ★

Make your friend the star of her own personalised novel! You could even feature in the story, too. Why not type it up and print it out, then add a cover and illustrations? This is such a fun gift – both to give, and to receive!

♡ BIRTHDAY QUIZ! ♡

Jacqueline's books are full of birthdays! Test yourself with this quiz. The answers are at the back of the book!

1. What is Tracy Beaker's birthday?

2. Which of the *Double Act* twins was born first?

3. In *The Worst Thing About My Sister*, whose birthday party does Marty really not want to go to?

4. In *Sleepovers*, all the girls in the Alphabet Club have different themes for their birthdays. Which girl has a picnic theme?

5. And which *Sleepovers* character does Daisy buy a special set of metallic pens for?

6. In *Queenie*, Elsie tells the other children in the hospital ward a story about the Land of Birthdays. What does Elsie wear in this land?

7. Elsie and the other children also pretend to play Pass the Parcel. What special present does Elsie give to Gillian?

8. Which character has a special profiterole tower instead of a birthday cake?

9. What is Jacqueline Wilson's birthday?

♡ BIRTHDAY PUZZLES ♡

★ FIND THE WORDS ★

How many words can you make from the letters below?

B I R T H D A Y C A K E

Why not challenge your friends and see how many you can find in three minutes?

Here are a few to get you started:
CAT
BRIDE

★ UNSCRAMBLE THE WORDS ★

Can you identify these traditional birthday games?

PLACER HAT PESS

CALM TUSSUI EATS

PINNI GLOSS EEL

LAMB DUFF BLINNS

PLONG BIBB PEA

(You'll find all the answers on the last page of this Journal!)

★ CROSSWORD ★

Tuck in to the tastiest crossword ever! Here's a hint: every word is a snack or treat you'd eat at a birthday party.

DOWN:

1. Usually eaten when watching a film – and can be very noisy to make!

2. Made from sugar and butter, this can be a sticky sauce or a sweet on its own.

3. A crunchy snack made from potatoes. Flavours include salt and vinegar and prawn cocktail!

4. A sugary, buttery Scottish biscuit.

5. A hot savoury treat, first made in Italy, and served in slices.

6. The perfect accompaniment to warm puddings like apple crumble. And yellow!

7. Wobbly, sweet, and usually eaten with ice cream.

8. A chocolate-flavoured treat, first made in America. You'll find a yummy recipe in this Journal!

ACROSS:

3. You might eat this served on a stick with pineapple al a party. Or it's a tasty sandwich filling!

5. A light, sweet dessert made from meringues, and named after a famous ballerina.

9. Fluffy pastry balls filled with cream and drizzled with chocolate – yum.

10. A fruity treat used in sandwiches and cakes, and spread on scones, crumpets or toast!

♡ WHAT'S YOUR ♡
STAR SIGN?

The day you were born tells you what star sign you are.
Find yours below — you might know it already!

★ CAPRICORN: The Goat ★
(22nd December — 19th January)

As a Capricorn, one of the earth signs, you're a high
achiever and might do really well at school. You're
hard-working and you may be quite quiet and shy —
but you're determined to meet your goals.

★ AQUARIUS: The Water-Carrier ★
(20th January — 18th February)

If you're an Aquarius, you're an air sign, and your
best gift is how friendly you are. You're interested
in helping and understanding other people, and
you can be very tolerant and patient.

★ PISCES: The Fishes ★
(19th February — 20th March)

Pisces is a water sign, and if you're a Pisces you're thought
to be a real daydreamer! You're also kind, compassionate,
and artistic, but you may not be very practical.

★ ARIES: The Ram ★
(21st March – 20th April)

Aries is one of the fire signs. If you're an Aries, you might be full of energy, very brave, and ready for any challenge! You might also be a natural leader. You also like to get your own way!

★ TAURUS: The Bull ★
(21st April – 20th May)

As a Taurus, one of the earth signs, you might be a reliable, peaceful person who likes home comforts. You're also thought to be very practical and patient – a very good friend.

★ GEMINI: The Twins ★
(21st May – 21st June)

Gemini is an air sign, and as a Gemini you're very sociable, love to be around other people – and like to be the centre of attention! Geminis are believed to love travelling.

★ CANCER: The Crab ★
(22nd June – 22nd July)

Cancer is a water sign. If you're a Cancer, you might be shy and sensitive, but you're extremely loyal and loving. Your friends and family are very important to you, and you may be quite protective of them.

★ LEO: The Lion ★
(23rd July – 22nd August)

Leo is one of the fire signs, and Leos are known for being confident, excellent leaders, and for having lots of good ideas. As a Leo, you're also very loving – but you can be easily hurt by arguments, or if someone disagrees with you.

★ VIRGO: The Maiden ★
(23rd August – 22nd September)

As an earth sign, Virgos are often calm, quiet, creative people who love animals and nature. If you're a Virgo, you might be quite shy, and enjoy your own company – but you're a very caring friend too.

★ LIBRA: The Scales ★
(23rd September – 22nd October)

Libra is an air sign, and if you're a Libran you can be a very affectionate, charming person, who loves to be around friends. You might find it difficult to make decisions sometimes, because you're so thoughtful.

★ SCORPIO: The Scorpion ★
(23rd October – 21st November)

As a Scorpio, you're a water sign and you're thought to be a very wise, sensitive person. You might be quite secretive, and you're a very good judge of character.

★ SAGITTARIUS: The Archer ★
(22nd November – 21st December)

Sagittarius is a fire sign, and you're thought to be an adventurous person who loves travelling, meeting new people and trying new things. You're very positive, and also very curious.

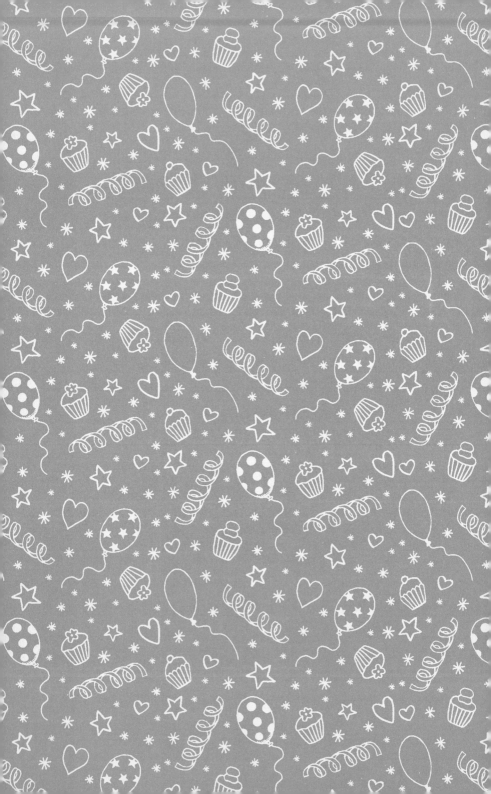

JANUARY

I go into the kitchen and peer into the fridge,
wondering what we can have for party food.
Well, we can have ice cream for a start.

Little Darlings

MY JANUARY BIRTHDAYS

Who do you know with a
birthday in January?

_____

_____

_____

_____

_____

_____

_____

_____

_____

_____

_____

_____

_____

_____

_____

_____

_____

FAMOUS JANUARY BIRTHDAYS!

Did you know all these people have January birthdays?

★ Kate Middleton, Duchess of Cambridge (9th January) ★

★ Anne Bronte, author (17th January) ★

★ A. A. Milne, author (18th January) ★

★ Gary Barlow, singer (20th January) ★

★ Lewis Carroll, author (27th January) ★

★ Jessica Ennis, athlete (28th January) ★

♡ BIRTHDAYS I WENT ♡ TO IN JANUARY

It was _____ 's birthday on _____ January

They were _____ years old

We celebrated their birthday at _____

_____

These were the other people there _____

_____

We ate _____

_____

We listened to _____

_____

The present I gave them was _____

_____

Other presents they received _____

_____

The best thing about this birthday was _____

_____

_____

_____

_____

It was _____ 's birthday on _____ January

They were _____ years old

We celebrated their birthday at _____

_____

These were the other people there _____

_____

We ate _____

_____

We listened to _____

_____

The present I gave them was _____

_____

Other presents they received _____

_____

The best thing about this birthday was _____

_____

_____

_____

_____

_____

_____

It was _____ 's birthday on _____ January

They were _____ years old

We celebrated their birthday at _____
_____

These were the other people there _____
_____

We ate _____
_____

We listened to _____
_____

The present I gave them was _____
_____

Other presents they received _____
_____

The best thing about this birthday was _____
_____
_____
_____
_____
_____

A PARTY IDEA FOR JANUARY

Why not try a fancy dress party with a twist?
Choose any letter of the alphabet — it could
be the first letter of your name, for example.
Then, everyone has to come dressed as
something beginning with that letter!

Amy

Bella

Chloe

Daisy

Emily

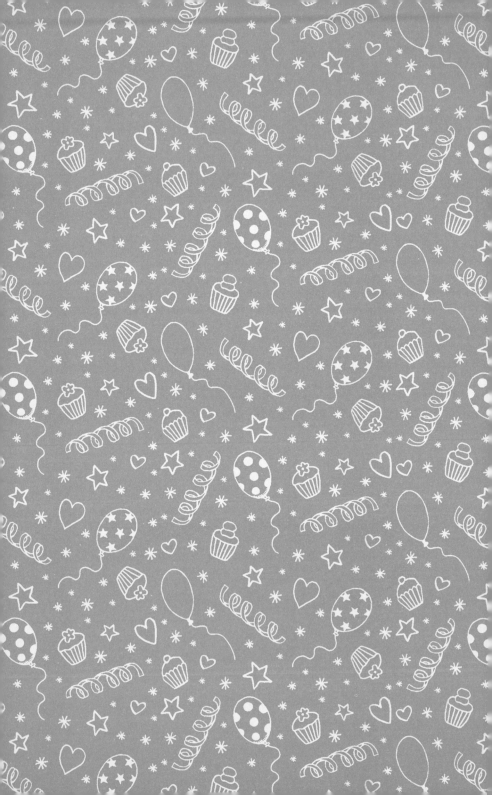

FEBRUARY

There were bowls of trifle and tiramisú, and a special ice-cream cake, and a raspberry pavlova, and a cheesecake, and a profiterole tower, and an enormous birthday cake with a picture of a ballet dancer in a lilac dress.

The Worst Thing About My Sister

MY FEBRUARY BIRTHDAYS

Who do you know with a
birthday in February?

_____

_____

_____

_____

_____

_____

_____

_____

_____

_____

_____

_____

_____

_____

FAMOUS FEBRUARY BIRTHDAYS!

Did you know all these people have
February birthdays?

★ Charles Dickens, author (7th February) ★

★ Taylor Lautner, actor (11th February) ★

★ Kelly Rowland, singer (11th February) ★

★ Ed Sheeran, singer (17th February) ★

★ Dakota Fanning, actress (23rd February) ★

♡ BIRTHDAYS I WENT ♡
TO IN FEBRUARY

It was _____ 's birthday on ____ February

They were _____ years old

We celebrated their birthday at _____

_____

These were the other people there _____

_____

We ate _____

_____

We listened to _____

_____

The present I gave them was _____

_____

Other presents they received _____

_____

The best thing about this birthday was _____

_____

_____

_____

_____

It was _____ 's birthday on ____ February

They were _____ years old

We celebrated their birthday at _____
_____

These were the other people there _____
_____

We ate _____
_____

We listened to _____
_____

The present I gave them was _____
_____

Other presents they received _____
_____

The best thing about this birthday was _____
_____
_____

_____
_____
_____

_____

It was _____ 's birthday on _____ February

They were _____ years old

We celebrated their birthday at _____

_____

These were the other people there _____

_____

We ate _____

_____

We listened to _____

_____

The present I gave them was _____

_____

Other presents they received _____

_____

The best thing about this birthday was _____

_____

_____

_____

_____

_____

A PARTY IDEA FOR FEBRUARY

How about a circus-themed party? Decorate your living room in red, yellow and gold, and ask everyone to dress as their favourite circus performer. Read *Hetty Feather*, *Sapphire Battersea* or *Emerald Star* for some ideas!

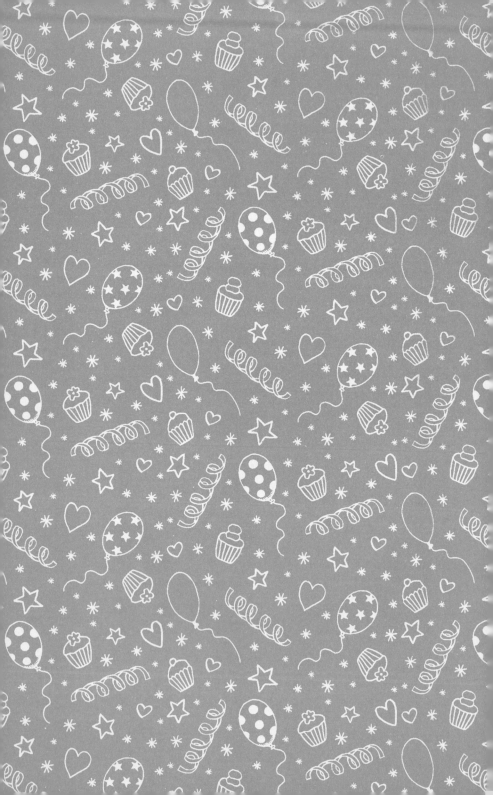

MARCH

'No, I said, it's the Land of Birthdays.
And I'm climbing the ladder, stepping through
the clouds, and suddenly it's brilliant sunshine,
and so warm! The trees are hung with those little
lights you get on Christmas trees, with huge
pink balloons tied to all the branches.'

Queenie

MY MARCH BIRTHDAYS

Who do you know with a
birthday in March?

_____

_____

_____

_____

_____

_____

_____

_____

_____

_____

_____

_____

FOR MY
TRACY x

FAMOUS MARCH BIRTHDAYS!

Did you know all these people have
March birthdays?

★ Justin Bieber, singer (1st March) ★

★ Andrew Lloyd Webber, composer (22nd March) ★

★ Reese Witherspoon, actress (22nd March) ★

★ Harry Houdini, magician (24th March) ★

★ Keira Knightley, actress (26th March) ★

★ Lady Gaga, singer (28th March) ★

♡ BIRTHDAYS I WENT ♡
TO IN MARCH

It was _____ 's birthday on _____ March

They were _____ years old

We celebrated their birthday at _____
_____

These were the other people there _____
_____

We ate _____
_____

We listened to _____
_____

The present I gave them was _____
_____

Other presents they received _____
_____

The best thing about this birthday was _____
_____
_____
_____
_____

It was _____ 's birthday on _____ March

They were _____ years old

We celebrated their birthday at _____

_____

These were the other people there _____

_____

We ate _____

_____

We listened to _____

_____

The present I gave them was _____

_____

Other presents they received _____

_____

The best thing about this birthday was _____

_____

_____

_____

_____

_____

It was _____ 's birthday on _____ March

They were _____ years old

We celebrated their birthday at _____
_____

These were the other people there _____
_____

We ate _____
_____

We listened to _____
_____

The present I gave them was _____
_____

Other presents they received _____
_____

The best thing about this birthday was _____
_____
_____
_____
_____
_____

A PARTY IDEA FOR MARCH

How about a baking party? Everyone will need to bring an apron, and you'll need to ask a parent or grandparent for help! Pick your favourite cookie, cupcake or brownie recipes, and ask everyone to help with measuring, mixing and decorating. Make sure all your guests take home a treat in their party bag!

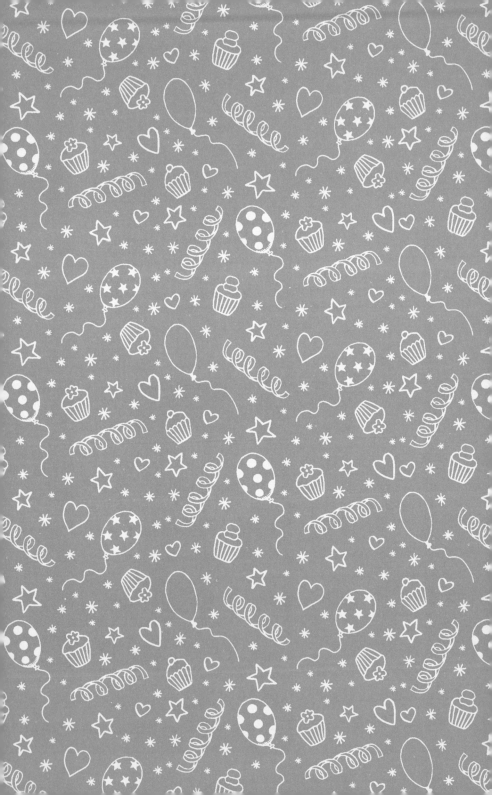

APRIL

'Guess what!' said Amy. 'It's my birthday next
week and my mum says I can invite all my
special friends for a sleepover party.'

Sleepovers

MY APRIL BIRTHDAYS

Who do you know with a
birthday in April?

FAMOUS APRIL BIRTHDAYS!

Did you know all these people have
April birthdays?

★ Hans Christian Andersen, fairy-tale author (2nd April) ★

★ Leona Lewis, singer (3rd April) ★

★ Kristen Stewart, actress (9th April) ★

★ Emma Watson, actress (15th April) ★

★ Leonardo da Vinci, artist and inventor (15th April) ★

★ Queen Elizabeth (21st April) ★

★ Charlotte Bronte, author (21st April) ★

★ William Shakespeare, playwright (23rd April) ★

♡ BIRTHDAYS I WENT ♡ TO IN APRIL

It was _____ 's birthday on _____ April

They were _____ years old

We celebrated their birthday at _____

_____

These were the other people there _____

_____

We ate _____

_____

We listened to _____

_____

The present I gave them was _____

_____

Other presents they received _____

_____

The best thing about this birthday was _____

_____

_____

_____

_____

It was _____ 's birthday on _____ April

They were _____ years old

We celebrated their birthday at _____

_____

These were the other people there _____

_____

We ate _____

_____

We listened to _____

_____

The present I gave them was _____

_____

Other presents they received _____

_____

The best thing about this birthday was _____

_____

_____

_____

_____

_____

_____

It was _____ 's birthday on _____ April

They were _____ years old

We celebrated their birthday at _____

_____

These were the other people there _____

_____

We ate _____

_____

We listened to _____

_____

The present I gave them was _____

_____

Other presents they received _____

_____

The best thing about this birthday was _____

_____

_____

_____

_____

_____

A PARTY IDEA
FOR APRIL

How about a sleepover? It's one of the most
fun ways to celebrate a birthday with lots of
very good friends! And there are some brilliant
tips on how to have the best sleepover ever
in this Journal.

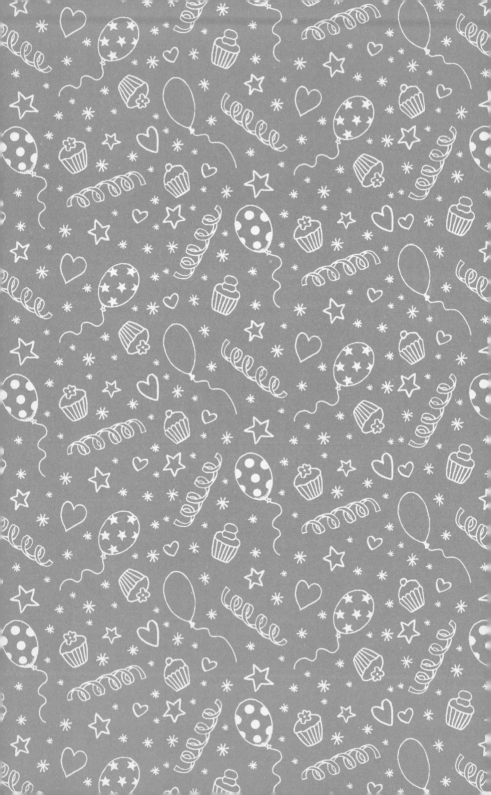

MAY

Guess what Cam bought for tea! A birthday cake,
quite a big one, with jam and cream inside.
The top was just plain white, but she took some
of my Smarties and spelt out T.B. on the top.

The Story of Tracy Beaker

MY MAY BIRTHDAYS

Who do you know with a
birthday in May?

_____

_____

_____

_____

_____

_____

_____

_____

_____

_____

_____

_____

_____

_____

_____

_____

FAMOUS MAY BIRTHDAYS!

Did you know all these people have May birthdays?

★ David Beckham, footballer (2nd May) ★

★ Adele, singer (5th May) ★

★ Tracy Beaker (8th May) ★

★ Florence Nightingale, nurse (12th May) ★

★ Robert Pattinson, actor (13th May) ★

★ Sir Arthur Conan Doyle, author (22nd May) ★

★ Helena Bonham Carter, actress (26th May) ★

♡ BIRTHDAYS I WENT ♡ TO IN MAY

It was _____ 's birthday on _____ May

They were _____ years old

We celebrated their birthday at _____

_____

These were the other people there _____

_____

We ate _____

_____

We listened to _____

_____

The present I gave them was _____

_____

Other presents they received _____

_____

The best thing about this birthday was _____

_____

_____

_____

_____

It was _____ 's birthday on _____ May

They were _____ years old

We celebrated their birthday at _____

_____

These were the other people there _____

_____

We ate _____

_____

We listened to _____

_____

The present I gave them was _____

_____

Other presents they received _____

_____

The best thing about this birthday was _____

_____

_____

_____

_____

_____

_____

It was _____ 's birthday on _____ May

They were _____ years old

We celebrated their birthday at _____

_____

These were the other people there _____

_____

We ate _____

_____

We listened to _____

_____

The present I gave them was _____

_____

Other presents they received _____

_____

The best thing about this birthday was _____

_____

_____

_____

_____

_____

A PARTY IDEA
FOR MAY

How about a zoo party? Ask everyone to
pick their favourite animal, and come in costume!
You can play a soundtrack of animal noises in the
background, serve cookies and biscuits cut into
the shape of paw-prints, and you could even ask
your mum or dad or an older brother or sister
to dress as a zoo-keeper!

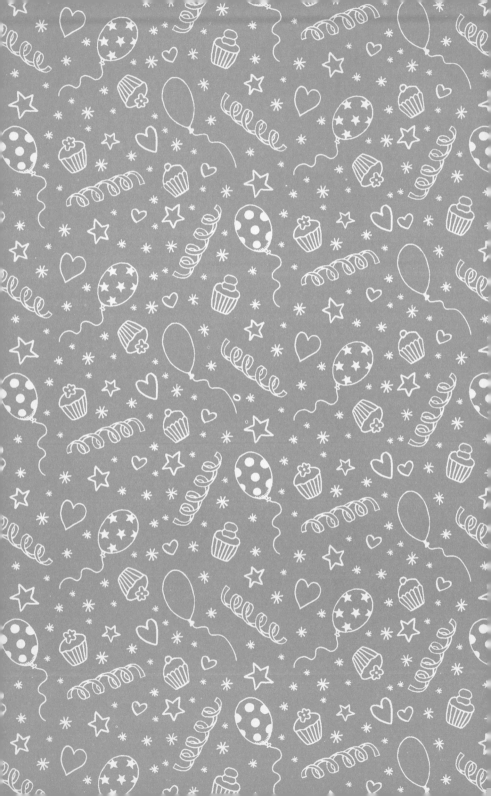

JUNE

I had a special birthday breakfast of croissants and
cherry jam and hot chocolate — yummy yummy.

Sleepovers

MY JUNE BIRTHDAYS

Who do you know with a
birthday in June?

_____
_____
_____
_____
_____
_____
_____
_____
_____
_____
_____
_____
_____
_____

FAMOUS JUNE BIRTHDAYS!

Did you know all these people have
June birthdays?

★ Marilyn Monroe, actress (1st June) ★

★ Rafael Nadal, tennis player (3rd June) ★

★ Angelina Jolie, actress (4th June) ★

★ Johnny Depp, actor (9th June) ★

★ Judy Garland, actress (10th June) ★

★ Anne Frank, author (12th June) ★

★ Prince William (21st June) ★

★ Cheryl Cole, singer (30th June) ★

♡ BIRTHDAYS I WENT ♡ TO IN JUNE

It was _____ 's birthday on _____ June

They were _____ years old

We celebrated their birthday at _____
_____

These were the other people there _____
_____

We ate _____
_____

We listened to _____
_____

The present I gave them was _____
_____

Other presents they received _____
_____

The best thing about this birthday was _____
_____
_____
_____
_____

It was _____ 's birthday on _____ June

They were _____ years old

We celebrated their birthday at _____

_____

These were the other people there _____

_____

We ate _____

_____

We listened to _____

_____

The present I gave them was _____

_____

Other presents they received _____

_____

The best thing about this birthday was _____

_____

_____

_____

_____

_____

_____

It was _____ 's birthday on _____ June

They were _____ years old

We celebrated their birthday at _____

_____

These were the other people there _____

_____

We ate _____

_____

We listened to _____

_____

The present I gave them was _____

_____

Other presents they received _____

_____

The best thing about this birthday was _____

_____

_____

_____

_____

_____

_____

A PARTY IDEA
FOR JUNE

How about a picnic party? If you have a June birthday, take advantage of the sunshine and warm weather, and head into the garden or to the park. Remember to bring blankets, paper cups and plates, and fun activities – balls, skipping ropes and hula-hoops!

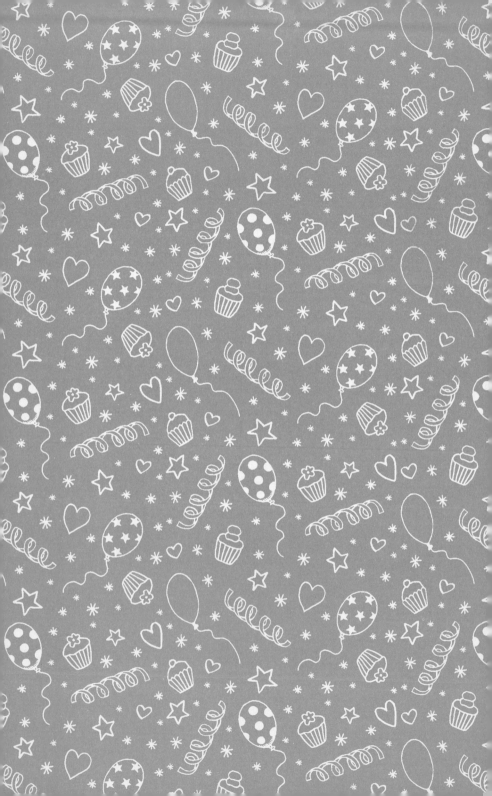

JULY

'My party's going to be extra specially-special,'
said Bella. 'We're all going swimming. My birthday
cake's going to have blue icing because it's in
the shape of a swimming pool.'

Sleepovers

MY JULY BIRTHDAYS

Who do you know with a birthday in July?

_____

_____

_____

_____

_____

_____

_____

_____

_____

_____

_____

_____

_____

FAMOUS JULY BIRTHDAYS!

Did you know all these people have
July birthdays?

★ Tom Hanks, actor (9th July) ★

★ Selena Gomez, actress and singer (22nd July) ★

★ Daniel Radcliffe, actor (23rd July) ★

★ Beatrix Potter, author (28th July) ★

★ Emily Bronte, author (30th July) ★

J. K. Rowling, author (31st July) ★

♡ BIRTHDAYS I WENT ♡ TO IN JULY

It was _____ 's birthday on _____ July

They were _____ years old

We celebrated their birthday at _____

_____

These were the other people there _____

_____

We ate _____

_____

We listened to _____

_____

The present I gave them was _____

_____

Other presents they received _____

_____

The best thing about this birthday was _____

_____

_____

_____

_____

It was _____ 's birthday on _____ July

They were _____ years old

We celebrated their birthday at _____

_____

These were the other people there _____

_____

We ate _____

_____

We listened to _____

_____

The present I gave them was _____

_____

Other presents they received _____

_____

The best thing about this birthday was _____

_____

_____

_____

_____

_____

_____

It was _____ 's birthday on _____ July

They were _____ years old

We celebrated their birthday at _____

_____

These were the other people there _____

_____

We ate _____

_____

We listened to _____

_____

The present I gave them was _____

_____

Other presents they received _____

_____

The best thing about this birthday was _____

_____

_____

_____

_____

_____

A PARTY IDEA FOR JULY

Make a splash on your birthday with a swimming
party, like Bella in *Sleepovers*! Or, if you have
a garden, you could try a paddling-pool party?
Make sure all your friends bring a swimming
costume, a towel and dry clothes!

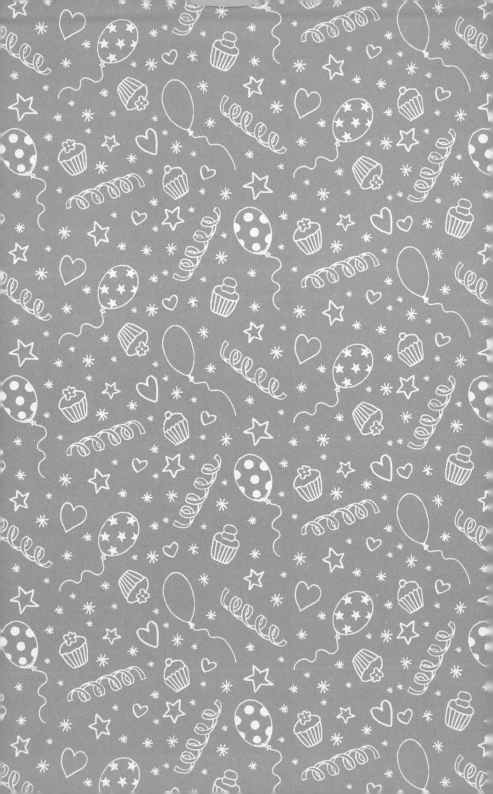

AUGUST

'It's a dance party. It's being held at Alisha's
dancing school. Alisha's mum told me all about it.
It's going to be like a very junior prom.'

The Worst Thing About My Sister

MY AUGUST
BIRTHDAYS

Who do you know with a
birthday in August?

_____

_____

_____

_____

_____

_____

_____

_____

_____

_____

_____

_____

_____

_____

_____

_____

_____

FAMOUS AUGUST BIRTHDAYS!

Did you know all these people have
August birthdays?

★ Nick Sharratt (9th August) ★

★ Madonna, singer (16th August) ★

★ Usain Bolt, athlete (21st August) ★

★ Rupert Grint, actor (24th August) ★

★ Jack Black, actor (28th August) ★

★ Lea Michele, actress (29th August) ★

♡ BIRTHDAYS I WENT ♡ TO IN AUGUST

It was _____ 's birthday on _____ August

They were _____ years old

We celebrated their birthday at _____
_____

These were the other people there _____
_____

We ate _____
_____

We listened to _____
_____

The present I gave them was _____
_____

Other presents they received _____
_____

The best thing about this birthday was _____
_____
_____
_____
_____

It was _____'s birthday on _____ August

They were _____ years old

We celebrated their birthday at _____

_____

These were the other people there _____

_____

We ate _____

_____

We listened to _____

_____

The present I gave them was _____

_____

Other presents they received _____

_____

The best thing about this birthday was _____

_____

_____

_____

_____

_____

_____

_____

It was _____ 's birthday on _____ August

They were _____ years old

We celebrated their birthday at _____

_____

These were the other people there _____

_____

We ate _____

_____

We listened to _____

_____

The present I gave them was _____

_____

Other presents they received _____

_____

The best thing about this birthday was _____

_____

_____

_____

_____

_____

A PARTY IDEA FOR AUGUST

How about a dance-themed party? All your friends can come as different types of dancer: ballet, flamenco, ballroom, jazz, disco. Then play your favourite music and invent a routine to perform together!

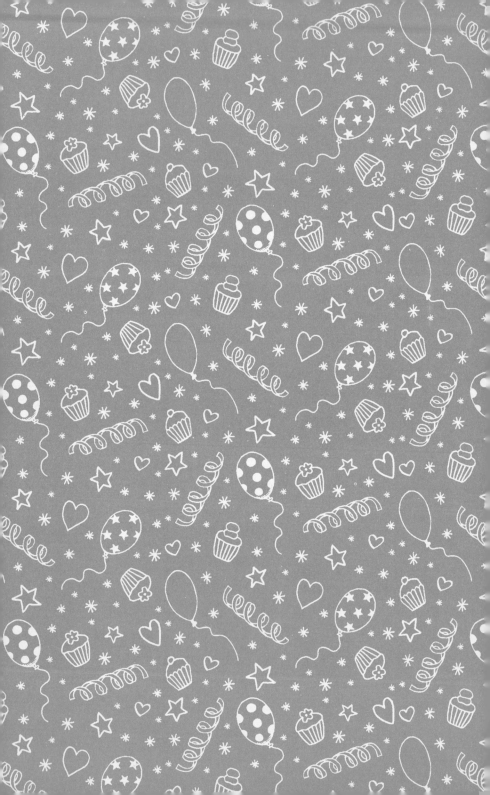

SEPTEMBER

There was a big bunch of pink and blue balloons tied
to the gate to show there was a party going on. The
living room glowed rose with pink fairy lights.

Cookie

MY SEPTEMBER BIRTHDAYS

Who do you know with a
birthday in September?

_____

_____

_____

_____

_____

_____

_____

_____

_____

_____

_____

_____

_____

_____

_____

FAMOUS SEPTEMBER BIRTHDAYS!

Did you know all these people have
September birthdays?

★ Beyonce Knowles, singer (4th September) ★

★ Fearne Cotton, TV presenter (9th September) ★

★ Roald Dahl, author (13th September) ★

★ Prince Harry (15th September) ★

★ Tom Felton, actor (22nd September) ★

♡ BIRTHDAYS I WENT ♡ TO IN SEPTEMBER

It was _____ 's birthday on __ September

They were _____ years old

We celebrated their birthday at _____
_____

These were the other people there _____
_____

We ate _____
_____

We listened to _____
_____

The present I gave them was _____
_____

Other presents they received _____
_____

The best thing about this birthday was _____
_____
_____
_____
_____

It was _____ 's birthday on __ September

They were _____ years old

We celebrated their birthday at _____

_____

These were the other people there _____

_____

We ate _____

_____

We listened to _____

_____

The present I gave them was _____

_____

Other presents they received _____

_____

The best thing about this birthday was _____

_____

_____

_____

_____

_____

_____

It was _____ 's birthday on __ September

They were _____ years old

We celebrated their birthday at _____
_____

These were the other people there _____
_____

We ate _____
_____

We listened to _____
_____

The present I gave them was _____
_____

Other presents they received _____
_____

The best thing about this birthday was _____
_____
_____
_____
_____
_____
_____

A PARTY IDEA FOR SEPTEMBER

What's your favourite colour? You could make that the theme of your birthday party! Whether it's pale pink, deep violet, bright orange or ruby red, ask your friends to dress in that colour and make party snacks to match!

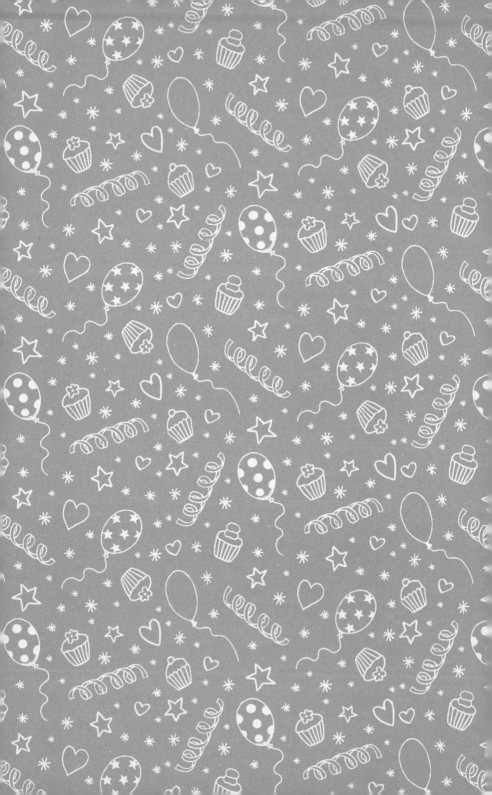

OCTOBER

Mum had always longed to give Jodie and me
a proper girly party, where we wore pretty dresses
and played old-fashioned games like Musical
Bumps and Pass the Parcel and ate sausages
on sticks and trifle and fairy cakes.

My Sister Jodie

MY OCTOBER BIRTHDAYS

Who do you know with a
birthday in October?

_____
_____
_____
_____
_____
_____
_____
_____
_____
_____
_____
_____
_____
_____
_____

FAMOUS OCTOBER BIRTHDAYS!

Did you know all these people have October birthdays?

★ Nicola Roberts, singer (5th October) ★

★ Simon Cowell, TV presenter (7th October) ★

★ Zac Efron, actor (18th October) ★

★ Pablo Picasso, artist (25th October) ★

★ Willow Smith, singer (31st October) ★

♡ BIRTHDAYS I WENT ♡ TO IN OCTOBER

It was _____ 's birthday on _____ October

They were _____ years old

We celebrated their birthday at _____
_____

These were the other people there _____
_____

We ate _____
_____

We listened to _____
_____

The present I gave them was _____
_____

Other presents they received _____
_____

The best thing about this birthday was _____
_____
_____
_____
_____

It was _____ 's birthday on _____ October

They were _____ years old

We celebrated their birthday at _____

_____

These were the other people there _____

_____

We ate _____

_____

We listened to _____

_____

The present I gave them was _____

_____

Other presents they received _____

_____

The best thing about this birthday was _____

_____

_____

_____

_____

_____

_____

It was _____ 's birthday on _____ October

They were _____ years old

We celebrated their birthday at _____

_____

These were the other people there _____

_____

We ate _____

_____

We listened to _____

_____

The present I gave them was _____

_____

Other presents they received _____

_____

The best thing about this birthday was _____

_____

_____

_____

_____

_____

_____

A PARTY IDEA FOR OCTOBER

There's nothing more fun than an old-fashioned party, with birthday games like Pass the Parcel, and a traditional birthday tea! It's a good excuse to dress up in your favourite sparkly party dress and for you and all your friends to be super girly together.

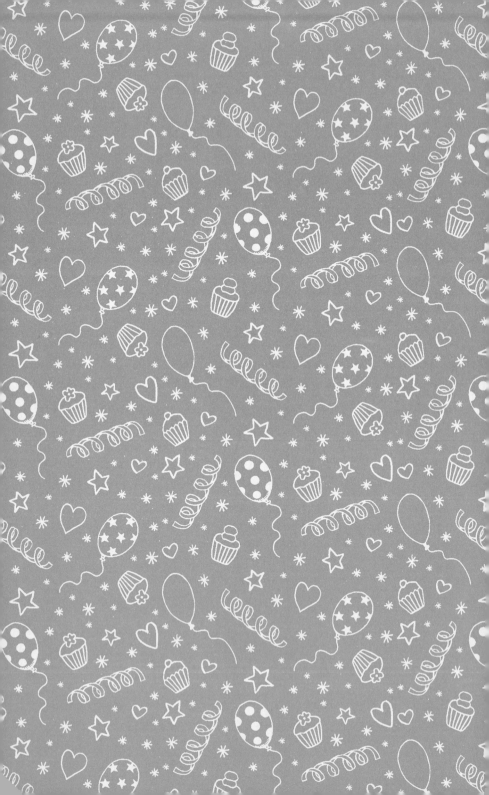

NOVEMBER

Louise had this really fantastic frock that she got a couple of years ago from some auntie. A real posh party frock with smocking and a flouncy skirt and its own sewn-in frilly white petticoat.

The Story of Tracy Beaker

MY NOVEMBER BIRTHDAYS

Who do you know with a
birthday in November?

_____
_____
_____
_____
_____
_____
_____
_____
_____
_____
_____
_____
_____
_____
_____
_____

FOR MY
TRACY x

FAMOUS NOVEMBER BIRTHDAYS!

Did you know all these people have November birthdays?

★ Robert Lewis Stevenson, author (13th November) ★

★ Prince Charles (14th November) ★

★ Miley Cyrus, actress and singer (23rd November) ★

★ Frances Hodgson Burnett, author (24th November) ★

★ Louisa May Alcott, author (29th November) ★

♡ BIRTHDAYS I WENT ♡ TO IN NOVEMBER

It was _____ 's birthday on __ November

They were _____ years old

We celebrated their birthday at _____

_____

These were the other people there _____

_____

We ate _____

_____

We listened to _____

_____

The present I gave them was _____

_____

Other presents they received _____

_____

The best thing about this birthday was _____

_____

_____

_____

_____

It was _____ 's birthday on __ November

They were _____ years old

We celebrated their birthday at _____

_____

These were the other people there _____

_____

We ate _____

_____

We listened to _____

_____

The present I gave them was _____

_____

Other presents they received _____

_____

The best thing about this birthday was _____

_____

_____

_____

_____

_____

_____

It was _____ 's birthday on __ November

They were _____ years old

We celebrated their birthday at _____
_____

These were the other people there _____
_____

We ate _____
_____

We listened to _____
_____

The present I gave them was _____
_____

Other presents they received _____
_____

The best thing about this birthday was _____
_____
_____
_____
_____
_____

A PARTY IDEA FOR NOVEMBER

Try a movie party – pick two or three of your favourite films, make a huge bowl of popcorn, and invite your friends over to watch them with you. You could even act out your favourite scenes!

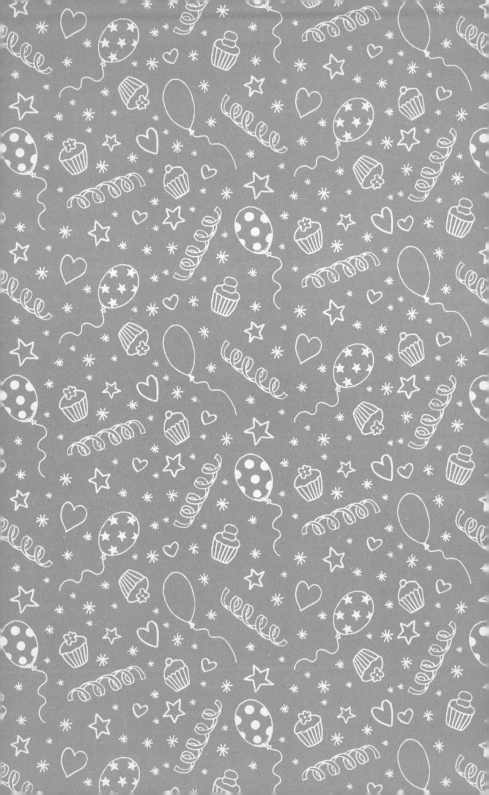

DECEMBER

I had my first birthday. Biddy and Harry gave me a book – not a baby's board book, a proper child's history book, though it had lots of pictures. Biddy wrote in her elaborately neat handwriting: To our darling little Jacqueline on her first birthday, Love from Mummy and Daddy.

Jacky Daydream

MY DECEMBER BIRTHDAYS

Who do you know with a
birthday in December?

_____

_____

_____

_____

_____

_____

_____

_____

_____

_____

_____

_____

_____

_____

FAMOUS DECEMBER BIRTHDAYS!

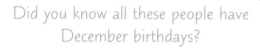

Did you know all these people have
December birthdays?

★ Jacqueline Wilson (17th December) ★

★ Walt Disney, filmmaker (5th December) ★

★ Taylor Swift, singer (13th December) ★

★ Vanessa Hudgens, actress (14th December) ★

★ Quentin Blake, illustrator (16th December) ★

★ Steven Spielberg, director (18th December) ★

★ Stephenie Meyer, author (24th December) ★

★ Dame Maggie Smith, actress (28th December) ★

♡ BIRTHDAYS I WENT ♡ TO IN DECEMBER

It was _____ 's birthday on ___ December

They were _____ years old

We celebrated their birthday at _____
_____

These were the other people there _____
_____

We ate _____
_____

We listened to _____
_____

The present I gave them was _____
_____

Other presents they received _____
_____

The best thing about this birthday was _____
_____
_____
_____
_____

It was _____ 's birthday on __ December

They were _____ years old

We celebrated their birthday at _____

_____

These were the other people there _____

_____

We ate _____

_____

We listened to _____

_____

The present I gave them was _____

_____

Other presents they received _____

_____

The best thing about this birthday was _____

_____

_____

_____

_____

_____

_____

It was _____ 's birthday on ___ December

They were _____ years old

We celebrated their birthday at _____

_____

These were the other people there _____

_____

We ate _____

_____

We listened to _____

_____

The present I gave them was _____

_____

Other presents they received _____

_____

The best thing about this birthday was _____

_____

_____

_____

_____

_____

A PARTY IDEA FOR DECEMBER

December is the perfect time of year for an
ice skating party! Ask your mum or dad to help
you find out where your local skating rink is.
Get wrapped up warm in your favourite hat, scarf
and gloves, and make sure there's plenty of hot
chocolate and warm muffins waiting for you
and your friends when you get home.

♡ MAKE A PHOTO ALBUM ♡

How many birthdays did you help celebrate
this year? What were your favourite moments
and memories? Collect together the best
birthday photos and stick them here!

CHECK OUT JACQUELINE WILSON'S OFFICIAL WEBSITE!

You'll find lots of fun stuff including games and amazing competitions. You can even customise your own page and start an online diary!

You'll find out all about Jacqueline in her monthly diary and tour blogs, as well as seeing her replies to fan mail. You can also chat to other fans on the message boards.

Join in today at
www.jacquelinewilson.co.uk

And to view the exciting book trailers including *Lily Alone*, *Sapphire Battersea* and *The Worst Thing About My Sister*, visit Jacqueline's official YouTube channel at
www.youtube.com/jacquelinewilson.tv

ALSO AVAILABLE BY JACQUELINE WILSON

THE JACQUELINE WILSON BIRTHDAY JOURNAL
A DOUBLEDAY BOOK 978 0 857 53306 7

First published in Great Britain by Corgi,
an imprint of Random House Children's Publishers UK
A Random House Group Company

Corgi edition published 2012
This edition published 2013

1 3 5 7 9 10 8 6 4 2

Set in Blueprint

RANDOM HOUSE CHILDREN'S PUBLISHERS UK
61–63 Uxbridge Road, London W5 5SA

www.randomhousechildrens.co.uk   www.totallyrandombooks.co.uk   www.randomhouse.co.uk

Addresses for companies within The Random House Group Limited
can be found at: www.randomhouse.co.uk/offices.htm

THE RANDOM HOUSE GROUP Limited Reg. No. 954009

A CIP catalogue record for this book is available from the British Library.

Printed and bound in China

The Random House Group Limited supports the Forest Stewardship Council (FSC®),
the leading international forest certification organization. Our books carrying the FSC label
are printed on FSC®-certified paper. FSC is the only forest certification scheme endorsed
by the leading environmental organizations, including Greenpeace. Our paper procurement
policy can be found at www.randomhouse.co.uk/environment.

MIX
Paper from
responsible sources
FSC® C020056

PARTY PUZZLE ANSWERS:
1. PASS THE PARCEL
2. MUSICAL STATUES
3. SLEEPING LIONS
4. BLIND MAN'S BLUFF
5. APPLE BOBBING
6. A PINK BALLET DRESS
7. A GRAMOPHONE
8. BEAUTY IN COOKIE
9. 17TH DECEMBER

BIRTHDAY QUIZ ANSWERS:
1. 8TH MAY 2. RUBY
3. ALISHA 4. EMILY 5. AMY